Gene Kemp was born in Wigginton, a small Midland village outside Tamworth, whose famous pigs she celebrates in the *Tamworth Pig Stories*, of which *Tamworth Pig Saves the Trees* is the second.

After several books about this wonderful pig and his friends, she broke new ground with her school story, *The Turbulent Term of Tyke Tiler*, which was awarded the Library Association's Carnegie Medal in 1978. In 1984 she was awarded an honorary Master of Arts degree in recognition of her achievement as a writer of children's books.

Gene Kemp now lives in Exeter. She is married with three children and has two grand-daughters.

ff

TAMWORTH PIG
SAVES THE TREES

Gene Kemp

Illustrated by Carolyn Dinan

faber and faber

LONDON · BOSTON

First published in 1973
by Faber and Faber Limited
3 Queen Square London WC1N 3AU
Published with 'The Prime of Tamworth Pig' in 1987
as *Tamworth Pig Stories*
Reprinted in Fanfares edition in 1980
This edition first published in 1989

Printed in Great Britain by
Richard Clay Ltd Bungay Suffolk

A CIP record for this book
is available from the British Library

ISBN 0-571-14186-2

Chapter One

————————————*————————————

It was Saturday and Thomas arose singing.

"No school. No school," he carolled through the house.

He pushed open the door of Daddy's and Mummy's bedroom.

"It's Saturday, Dad. You can lie in bed for a bit."

Dad opened a weary eye and reached out for the alarm clock at the side of the bed. He shook it incredulously.

"Why, it's only five to six."

"Yes, I know. I only came in to tell you, you didn't have to wake up early today, as it's Saturday."

Daddy groaned pitifully and pulled the bedclothes over his head.

"Go away, you horrible child," came a muffled cry.

Thomas trotted away, leaving the door open, not hearing the call behind him.

"And close the door!"

He was too busy shaking his head and muttering about the ingratitude of grown-ups, who never appreciated anything that one did for them. Still, Blossom should be ready to play by now.

Blossom, his sister, was a wonderful teller of tales

and inventor of games. Yesterday she had begun the story of Stringo, the little boy made of string, and Thomas wanted to hear more of it. He opened her door. Gentle snuffles whiffled through the quiet room. He took a running leap and landed with his knees on her soft form. It was always pleasant jumping on Blossom. She was so plump and comfortable, just like a pillow, he thought. He felt quite fond of her, but, strangely enough, she didn't seem fond of him. Flushed with sleep, brown eyes full of tears, she pushed and kicked him off the bed.

"I was having a wonderful dream and now you've spoilt it. Go away, you horrible boy!"

Hurt, he stared at her, then walked out of the room. He didn't like being told to go away twice like that. People were peculiar, he decided as he made his way down to the kitchen.

Breakfast was obviously hours away, so he helped himself to his favourite cereal, pouring nearly all the packet into the largest Pyrex bowl, the one his mother made apple pies in. Some cereal fell on the floor where it made an extremely pleasing, scrunchy noise under his feet.

"Scrunchy, munchy, chunchy, grunchy," he murmured contentedly.

The sugar bowl was almost empty, so he found the sugar bag and tore it open. This proved difficult at first, so he pulled extra hard and the bag split right down the side, spilling half on the table. He scooped this on to the floor and turned to get the milk. There was only a pint left and he must leave some for Mummy's early

8

cup of tea. A bargain offer of an inflatable boat on the cereal packet caught his eye and he proceeded to read it as he poured out the milk. When he looked down he was surprised to find he had used the whole pint. He tried to get some back into the bottle but it proved impossible, so he gave up, and started on his cereal, and soon the kitchen was filled with the noise of Thomas eating.

What next? A day of infinite possibilities lay ahead. He could climb a mountain, tame a lion, walk a tight-rope, score a goal for England. Contemplating all these, he went upstairs and flung his friends, the snoring Hedgecock and sniffling Mr. Rab, out of his bed. Hedgecock, as cantankerous and irritable as ever, snarled at him, while Mr. Rab, a long, thin rabbit wearing a red and white striped waistcoat and green bow tie, whimpered as he tried to climb back into warmth and comfort.

He whimpered even more when Thomas set up an indoor football game of his own invention, involving a very hard, tiny, rubber ball. He hated football. His skinny legs always got hurt. Poetry was the thing Mr. Rab loved best of all, and next to poetry, Thomas's sister Blossom and then Thomas. He didn't love Hedgecock at all.

Once aroused, Hedgecock played quite well, though sometimes the ball got lost among his feathery prickles. No one ever knew what Hedgecock really was, and as he became incredibly cross if anyone tried to find out, it remained a mystery. It was also difficult to discover what he actually liked as he grumbled so much about everything whatsoever, but he did enjoy counting and numbers, and utterly despised Mr. Rab and his poetry.

At half-time, Thomas decided the hanging bed-clothes were in the way, so he hauled them all off, dumped them in the bathroom next door, and continued with the game. Finally Thomas's team won six two. Hedgecock and Mr. Rab always let him win because if he lost he grew very angry and threw things and stamped and shouted. The game over, to Thomas's satisfaction and no loss of temper, he went to the window and looked out between the curtains.

The morning was thick and white like cotton wool. They could not even see the bottom of the garden. In a moment Thomas had hauled jeans and sweater over his pyjamas and pulled on the slippers he never wore in

the house. Urging Hedgecock and Mr. Rab before him, he hurried out into the mist, which thinned around them as they walked across the white lawn, leaving a green trail behind them. Spiders' webs clung wetly to their hands and faces.

"Season of mists and mellow fruitfulness," Mr. Rab cried suddenly in his special, high, poetry-reciting voice.

He stopped equally suddenly as Hedgecock kicked him.

"Can't we go anywhere without you reciting your rotten old poetry?"

"It's not fair. It's not fair. I love poetry. It's much better than your horrid counting. Why, you'd even count your own snores if you could."

"I don't snore," Hedgecock objected indignantly.

"Yes you do. You snore like . . . like ten thousand chain saws cutting down trees."

"I—do—not—snore."

"Oh, yes, you do."

Hedgecock kicked Mr. Rab much harder this time, so that he squealed.

"Shut up, you two," Thomas commanded. "We're going to see Tamworth Pig. I hope he's up and not asleep like everyone else."

Tamworth's favourite damson tree and Pig House, Tamworth's home, loomed unexpectedly out of the mist and there in the doorway stood the great pig himself, huge and golden, like some lesser sun. President of the Animals' Union, great campaigner for such causes as "Grow More Food and Eat Less Meat" (especially pork), he was the most famous pig in Britain and Thomas's friend and ally.

"Come in and have some Pig's Delight," he invited.

They went in and settled on the hay-strewn floor. Tamworth's home, which he refused to call a sty, was very comfortable and decorated with posters and photographs. A transistor radio stood on a handsome chest, both presents from the Vegetarian Society in gratitude for Tamworth's efforts to stop people eating meat. He had not succeeded yet, but he persevered. He

handed round a bag of Pig's Delight, a special sweet he had concocted for children which did not rot the teeth. It tasted delicious, rather like a mixture of chocolate, treacle, strawberries, mint, toffee and marsh-mallow.

"Thanks," Thomas muttered as he chewed. "I've brought you a cabbage. I picked it in the garden on the way here."

"Thank you, dear boy. You know how I appreciate a fine cabbage. And it's most welcome, for Mrs. Baggs, that extremely mean woman, who is supposed to feed

me, has not yet appeared with one of her inferior repasts."

"Now that you're famous and quite rich, I wonder you don't get someone kind to look after you. I wouldn't have her. Not after she tried to have you slaughtered."

"Oh, that doesn't worry me. She won't do that again and, after all, I do belong to Farmer Baggs. He's all right, a good, honest man, and I wouldn't want to upset him by changing things. What's more, I like it here."

Cabbage consumed, Tamworth sat back on his vast haunches. His eyes glittered and he wore a look of intense excitement. Thomas peered at him curiously.

"What's up?" he asked.

The giant pig tapped the floor with his neat little trotters. They all waited. At last he spoke in a deep voice.

"Last night I dreamed a dream. . . ."

"Like Joseph, you mean," put in Mr. Rab helpfully.

"Don't interrupt, you pink-nosed fool," Hedgecock snapped.

"In my dream, I saw the country below me."

"You were the ruler?"

It was Hedgecock interrupting this time. Mr. Rab pulled a face at him.

"Oh, no. I do not seek power. It would not be right for a pig to rule our country, though I should probably do no worse than some have done. No, the land was actually below me because I was flying over it in a kind of hovercraft."

"It must have been very strong to stand your weight."

Too late Mr. Rab put a hand over his mouth as though to push back his words, but Tamworth took no notice anyway. He was staring into the distance as though re-living his dream.

"And—and—dearest friends, there were no trees!"

His voice shook with emotion.

"No trees? What do you mean?" Thomas asked.

"There were no trees to be seen. They'd all disappeared, been cut down, torn up, burnt, destroyed.

There were no forests, no woods, no commons, no shady gardens, no tree-lined parks. All, all were gone, the oak and the elm, the ash and the holly. There was no shade from the sun, no shelter from the storm, no branches for birds to nest in, nor for children to climb. There were no apples in Autumn, no trees for Christmas."

He paused, tears in his eyes.

"Don't be upset. It was only a dream. I have nasty ones sometimes. Forget it," Thomas said.

"I can't forget it. It was a vision of the future. Every day trees are destroyed. Every day trees are dying. We must save the trees," Tamworth cried.

A loud neighing was heard as the head of Joe the Shire Horse pushed through the aperture cut specially for him.

"What be 'ee goin' on about now, Tamworth?" he asked in his slow voice. "I 'eard 'ee talkin' on and on. I come to tell 'ee that Mrs. Baggs is just a-settin' out with your grub."

"Then I'm off," Thomas said, for Mrs. Baggs was no friend of his.

He stroked Tamworth's upstanding, furry ears.

"Cheer up. You don't want to worry about rotten old dreams."

"Don't you understand? I must start a new campaign. 'Grow more Food' is going well now. I can take time off for this newer, greater cause. Save the trees! Save the trees!" Tamworth cried, going to the door and gazing into the mist.

"I can only see the damson tree in this lot, and I

haven't heard of anyone threatening to cut that down," Hedgecock muttered.

The clank of a pail was heard. Mrs. Baggs was approaching, so Thomas, Hedgecock and Mr. Rab vanished rapidly into the fog.

"Tamworth's off again," Thomas said to Blossom as he re-entered the kitchen.

She sat, scrubbed, pink and shining, behind a mound of toast. Blossom dearly loved food.

"And so is Mum. You want to look out," she replied, licking the melting butter off her fingers.

"Why, what have I done?"

"I think she said that you'd made more mess before breakfast than most children do in a day."

"Well, that's unfair. All I did was to come downstairs, bothering no one, get myself some grub and go out. What's wrong with that?"

"That's not what she said you did. And if I were you, I'd change those slippers before she sees them."

"You're not me, and I don't want you to be, you great, fat, stupid girl. I don't care about slippers. I want to tell you about Tamworth."

"What about him?"

"He's got a new cause. He wants to save the trees."

"Is that you, Thomas?"

Mummy's voice was calling and her feet approaching. Thomas dived under the table, but it was no use. He was soon discovered. So, too, were his slippers.

Chapter Two

❋

Blossom sat back with a sigh of satisfaction, having just completed a banner, a huge creation mounted on two broom handles painted gold. The design was simple, a white background with "SAVE THE TREES" emblazoned on it in green. She laid it carefully on the floor to dry, together with two small pennants which read, "Planta Seeda Day" and "Keep Britain Green".

"There!" she said.

"They're jolly nice. I wish I could have written a poem on one," Mr. Rab said enviously.

"No one would be able to read it being marched along on a banner. You'd do better to write a marching song."

Mollified, Mr. Rab began to sing:

> *"I think that I shall never see*
> *A poem lovely as a tree."*

"Somebody's already written that one," Hedgecock growled.

"Come and help me clear up all this mess," Blossom said, eyeing the paints, rags, brushes and jars.

She was alone. Everyone had deserted her. Sighing, she pushed all the painting paraphernalia into the nearest cupboard, and wandered into the garden, where the sun beamed down on the dahlias, the chrysanthemums and the last roses. Saint Luke's little summer had arrived, in October, with some of the sunniest days of the year, before the equinoctial gales arrived to blow away the soft warmth and the mists, making way for winter.

"Let's go out, Mummy," she said, poking her head round the kitchen door where Mummy was surrounded by a quantity of flour, eggs, butter and bowls. Thomas was helping himself to some strips of raw pastry.

"Leave it alone, Thomas. There'll be none left. No, Blossom, I can't go out just now. I must get a few things ready for those new people, the Postlewaithes. I've asked them to supper tonight so that they can meet some of our friends."

"I bet we'll only have toast for tea while you've got all this gorgeous grub. It's not fair. You're not much of a Mum, are you?"

"And you're not much of a son, are you? But we have to put up with you," Daddy said, coming in in his black, yellow, orange, green, pink and blue, accidentally-handpainted shirt. He had been decorating upstairs. He propelled Thomas through the door with a painted hand.

"A walk will do you good," he smiled firmly.

"Ugh," Thomas replied.

"Oh, come on, I'll race you to Pig House," Blossom cried.

Tamworth was indulging in an afternoon nap when they arrived panting. He opened half an eye, then closed it again.

20

"I've finished the 'Save the Trees' banners," Blossom whispered in his ear.

It flopped up and down, then Tamworth raised his enormous bulk.

"Thank you, indeed, Blossom. I've no doubt they're painted in your usual beautiful style. I've still got some of the posters you did for 'Grow More Food'."

"There were thirty-eight sausages on sticks," Hedge-cock announced suddenly for no apparent reason.

"Shush!" Thomas, Blossom and Mr. Rab exclaimed simultaneously, looking nervously at Tamworth, who hated any mention of sausages, pork or bacon or any of his future possibilities. Fortunately, he did not appear to have heard.

"Let's go conkering," Thomas suggested.

"Conquering what?" Hedgecock asked.

"Getting conkers, he means, stupid. You know, those brown nuts that grow on trees," Mr. Rab said.

He yelped as Hedgecock bashed him.

"Come on, then. Where shall we go?" Blossom asked, stroking Mr. Rab soothingly.

"The Tumbling Wood is the best place, I think. There are some very fine trees there. Wait, I'll get a basket," Tamworth said.

They ran, jumped and skipped over the stream where Thomas had once nearly drowned an entire mole colony, through the Rainbow Field, so named because of its curved shape, and over Hunter's Bridge on to the rough track that led to the Tumbling Wood, which covered the highest hill in the neighbourhood and so gave the wood its name, for the trees looked as if they were tumbling down the hillside.

"Look at those beautiful trees," Tamworth said.

They all looked, even Hedgecock. Leaves were brown and yellow and gold against the blue sky. Trunks shone silver.

"Oh, come on," grunted the bored Hedgecock.

There were too many trees for him to count and any other beauty meant nothing at all to him. They ran into the wood.

"There's hundreds of conkers," Thomas cried and, for a while, there was silence as they looked and scrambled under the leaves for the glossy, brown nuts.

Hedgecock counted furiously; Mr. Rab held up a particularly magnificent specimen.

"Isn't it a beauty? I bet a fairy polished this one."

Hedgecock nearly choked.

"Fairy poppycock. Huh! You know fairies aren't real. Not like us."

Thomas put the extra large conker in his pocket instead of the basket.

"It is a good one, though. I'll ask Mum to bake this one for me, then I can use it in the conker fights at school."

"We've got ninety-eight altogether," Hedgecock said.

"Two more, then, and that's enough," Tamworth ruled.

"I'm going to hit that one on that branch," Thomas shouted.

He threw up a short stick and missed. He flung the stick again with extra force and half the branch broke off, descending on the head of Mr. Rab, dancing below. He fell in a heap, thin little paws twitching feebly in the twigs and leaves.

"Oh, poor Mr. Rab," Blossom cried, flinging aside the branch.

There was a piteous groan.

"He's all right. Get up, stripy," Hedgecock snorted.

"His poor nose has gone white," Blossom exclaimed, investigating the frail form for breaks or sprains.

He sank back in her arms, relishing all the attention that was being showered upon him.

"Looks like a blooming corpse," Hedgecock agreed, peering closely. "No, he's coming round. His nose is going that nasty, pink, blancmange colour again."

Tamworth, too, inspected Mr. Rab and pronounced

him free from fatal injury, and Hedgecock pushed him
into a sitting position with his snout. Finally he was
ready to carry on.

Blossom found a good collection of old sweets in
her pockets, for she always believed in keeping some
in reserve in case of emergencies, and they wandered
slowly out of the wood, eating blackberries and boiled
sweets together, an interesting mixture.

Mr. Rab groaned carefully from time to time as
they went along, just in case anyone should forget
that he had been severely injured. Hedgecock was
pretending to suck from an acorn pipe. The path
turned sharply. Before them stood a huge machine—a
bulldozer!

24

Tamworth stopped short.

"I wonder what this machine is doing here? Surely they don't intend to use it in this wood. Why, it has stood here since the days of the Romans and earlier still. Thomas, my boy, I don't like the look of that bulldozer."

"Let's wreck it," Thomas suggested hopefully.

"Certainly not. No vandalism. Come, it's time to return home. I think I must prepare a speech this evening."

They walked on slowly, then Hedgecock suddenly stopped.

"What's that stupid animal doing now? What a nuisance he is!"

They all looked round but there was no sign of Mr. Rab, so they retraced their steps to where they last remembered seeing him.

"Come on, Mr. Rab. It's time to go," Thomas called.

There was no reply.

"Do you think he's all right?" Blossom asked anxiously.

"It's fatal to take him to the woods," Hedgecock sighed. "He always wants to join the real rabbits. I bet that's what he's done now. And if he finds any, they'll only make fun of him. They always do."

"Come on, Mr. Rab," Thomas called again.

Hedgecock grumbled on.

"He's got no sense at all. He never did have. I don't go gallivanting with hedgehogs. I only met one once, and I couldn't stand the fellow. He couldn't count at all. Didn't even know how many paws he'd got."

The others were busy searching behind every bush and tree as he went on talking.

"Let's all shout together," Blossom suggested.

"One—two—three—go!"

"MR. RAB!"

The words re-echoed round the woods.

A thin form hurried from behind an elderberry bush. It was Mr. Rab, looking both pleased and sheepish, injuries forgotten.

"So sorry. So sorry. So sorry," he squeaked.

"Stop apologizing and come on. Where did you get to?" Thomas said.

"I've found a friend. A friend! He liked me. He really did. I'm going to see him again. He's got the sweetest little burrow."

"What sort of friend is he? Not a weasel or someone like that?"

Tamworth's voice was anxious, for he had no faith in Mr. Rab's ability to choose the right sort of friend. Neither had anyone else.

"Oh, no. He's really a nice rabbit, but he has a funny way of talking because he's a Welsh rabbit."

"Lumme," Hedgecock exclaimed. "That's all we needed, Mr. Rab and a Welsh rabbit. I hope he doesn't turn into a fox's dinner."

"Don't be unkind. There's no reason why Mr. Rab shouldn't have a friend."

"I agree with you, Tamworth. We'll take you to see him again, Mr. Rab." Blossom smiled at the excited creature.

"Not if I can help it," Hedgecock snorted.

Tamworth looked at the setting sun.

"I think we'd better hurry," he said.

An early bedtime had been indicated for Thomas because he had a knack of wrecking social occasions and Mummy did not want her evening ruined. Blossom was to be allowed to stay up for a while, so Thomas was in a wicked mood.

"It's not fair," he muttered as he settled into bed with Hedgecock and Mr. Rab.

"She's older than you," Mr. Rab pointed out.

"Yes, but much stupider."

He wrapped himself in Num, his soft square of grey blanket that stayed under the pillow and only came out at night. Very few friends were allowed to see Num.

Downstairs the Postlewaithes had arrived, eager to be friendly. They had no children of their own.

"I'd love to meet your little boy, too," Mrs. Postlewaithe cooed after she had been introduced to Blossom. "Can't I just peep at him in bed?"

"No," Daddy said.

"Oh, I know you don't really mean that. I'll just creep up on my own."

"I shouldn't bother," Daddy said, but he was weakening. Mrs. Postlewaithe was very pretty.

"I'll find the door," she said with a smile and tripped away.

Daddy put down his glass and followed. She found the right door, the one with all the finger marks on it,

27

and peeped in. A small boy with very untidy hair, covered in an old, grey blanket, glared back at her. Six or seven spikes protruded from his mouth.

"Oh dear! Oh, you poor child. I didn't know you were afflicted. Whatever's wrong?"

She ran towards the bed.

Thomas, who hated anyone to see Num, snatched at it furiously to stuff it under the pillow, snarling through the sausages on sticks in his mouth. A wide

assortment of peanuts, olives, cheese biscuits and rolls, all in very crumbled condition, fell on the floor as Daddy arrived through the door.

Downstairs, Mummy exclaimed to the dutifully helpful Blossom:

"Why, half the food's disappeared!"

Much later, Hedgecock looked out cautiously from his blanket of knitted squares.

"It's all right now. They're making a lot of noise downstairs. It's a good job that female person was there or it would have been much worse."

"Yes," Thomas agreed. "Sing the bedtime song, Mr. Rab. I need it after Daddy's thrown all my food in the bin. It's not fair. All that food for them but nothing for me."

Mr. Rab sang the song he had made up long ago when Thomas was little.

> "*Mr. Rab has gone to sleep*
> *Tucked in his tiny bed,*
> *He has curled up his little paws*
> *And laid down his sleepy head*."

"Ugh, what muck," Hedgecock growled.

Sometimes, these days, Thomas thought himself much too old for Mr. Rab's song, but when things went wrong, he still liked to hear it. It felt comforting, like Num.

But back at school, things went well, for the huge conker, soaked in vinegar, baked hard and polished, defeated all challengers and became Super Conk, the champion.

"I think it was because the fairies polished it specially," Mr. Rab said.

"Fairy poppycock," Hedgecock snapped.

"No, fairy thistledown," Mr. Rab sniggered.

He did not often make a little joke and he soon regretted it as Hedgecock kicked him sharply.

Chapter Three

———————————— ✳ ————————————

Blossom's banner was bright in the sunlight and the pennants fluttered in the gentle breeze. St. Luke's little summer had continued its fine efforts for several more days, which was a good omen for Tamworth Pig's march, now winding its way through the main street. It was to make a tour of the village to arrive at the ancient elm outside the 'Duck and Drake' where Tamworth was to make his speech.

The huge pig, bristles electric with excitement, led the way, followed closely by Blossom and Thomas carrying the two pennants, accompanied by Hedgecock and Mr. Rab. Next came the large banner borne aloft by Mrs. Postlewaithe and the Vicar's wife, who both believed in the importance of saving trees. They were followed by sixteen students from the local technical college and two archaeological students taking time off from a nearby dig. Nearly all Blossom's class had turned up to support the cause, but only one from Thomas's, a professor's son who had brought his father along. Both were very short-sighted, and thought the march was in aid of impoverished deep-sea fishermen.

Many animals came from the surrounding country-side, including one on a visit from Cornwall. Joe the Shire Horse, Barry McKenzie Goat and Fanny Cow brought up the rear of the procession to lend backs should anyone require aid and assistance along the way. Ethelberta Everready, the many-egg-laying hen, fluttered up and down the marching column, squawking happily. She loved any sort of goings on.

Thomas was tense and on the alert. All week he had endured taunts and jeers from Lurcher Dench and Christopher Robin Baggs, his old enemies, and had listened to threats of what they would do to the march. They would wreck it, they said. They would cause a riot. Eyes swivelling grimly from left to right, Thomas kept a look-out for all possible places of ambush.

P.C. Cubbins was also on the alert, walking along beside the procession. Fond as he was of Thomas and even fonder of dear Blossom, he was not at all sure that he approved of the whole business. The Vicar's wife was there, which lent it a respectable air but, still, you never knew. Many riots had been caused by people with the best of intentions.

On the other side of the column, P.C. Spriggs also marched along. His thoughts were quite straightforward. Any affair at all that had Thomas mixed up in it would run into trouble sooner or later. All he had to do was to await that moment.

But the march was moving peacefully along to the strains of a marching song composed by Mr. Rab.

"Save the trees!
Save the trees!
We're marching over here to save the trees.
Hand in hand and paw in paw,
Whether you've got two feet or four,
Raise your voice in a mighty roar
And save the trees!
Save the trees!"

The Vicar's wife's soprano soared magnificently above the rest as they turned the corner towards the elm tree where a small crowd awaited them. Thomas's eye ran over it warily, but it contained no enemies. He felt almost disappointed. He wouldn't have minded a scrap.

Tamworth mounted the small platform erected for him. Blossom watched anxiously, for she always worried about Tamworth's weight, but it seemed safe enough.

Tamworth's powerful voice rang out to the waiting crowd.

"Friends! Brothers! I come here today on behalf of other friends of ours. Beautiful, noble friends. Trees! And day by day, I regret to say, these beautiful, noble friends are being laid low."

He paused. Among the listening throng, there came a rustling and a ripple of movement eddying towards Tamworth as the crowd parted reluctantly to let someone pass to the foot of the platform. A small, plump, extremely pretty, pink and black pig seated herself directly below Tamworth and gazed at him adoringly with her soft, dark eyes. She was panting a little.

Tamworth looked down at her, swallowed, then continued with his speech.

"Brothers! Friends! We are gathered here to talk about. . . ."

His voice faltered and stopped. He gazed at the pretty pig.

"What's your name?" he asked hoarsely.

"Melanie," she answered, lowering her long eyelashes.

"Melanie," Tamworth repeated as though in a dream.

The crowd was starting to grow restless.

"Get on with the speech," Thomas hissed at Tamworth, who gulped, looked at the crowd and began again.

"Friends! Brothers! We are here. . . ."

"We've heard all that. Tell us something new," a heckler shouted.

Blossom knew all Tamworth's speech, as he had rehearsed it with her.

"Plant a seed a day, whenever you can," she whispered to him.

"Plant a seed," Tamworth echoed vaguely, staring like a lost pig at Melanie.

"O! Lumme! He's gone nuts," Hedgecock said to Thomas.

"Yes. We'll have to do something quick."

As though in answer to a prayer, and it must have been the first time that this was ever the answer to anyone's prayer, came the roar of motor bikes. The local "Hell's Angels", leather-jacketed, black-helmeted, led by Deadly Dench, Lurcher's even more ferocious elder brother, came rocketing down the road, driving straight for the band of tree-savers, who broke up, scattered and ran for safety.

Thomas, helpless and furious, watched from the shelter of the Post Office doorway as they roared back and forth, again and again, accompanied by ear-splitting revs, bangs and shrieks. Finally a police car, summoned by P.C. Spriggs, arrived on the scene and

the 'Angels' sped away to seek further entertainment elsewhere.

Thomas and Blossom emerged from their shelter, clutching their pennants still. All was deserted except for Tamworth Pig and Melanie gazing into each other's eyes, oblivious of the whole world. Thomas and Blossom also stared, Thomas in despair, Blossom beaming from ear to ear.

"Look at them," she breathed.

"I never thought it really happened," Hedgecock grunted. "And I'm very sorry to see it does."

"Love, love, love," Mr. Rab warbled happily.

"Shut up, you stripy fool. Can't you see we're in for trouble? This afternoon has been a failure in every way," Hedgecock said.

"A failure? You mean a disaster," Thomas groaned.

Chapter Four

———————————— * ————————————

Next day, the Autumn sunshine had gone at last as the gales roared over the land, blasting the bright flowers, stripping the trees, blustering, whistling, roaring.

"Summer's gone and we've come."

Thomas's thoughts were as stormy as the weather as he sat in the classroom putting the finishing touches to a papier mâché puppet he was making and, ever after, this particular puppet always had to play the villain because of the ferocity of his painted face.

His stomach ached and he wanted to cry but could not. Tamworth had always been there across the years, as long as he could remember, invariably wise and kind and splendid, a true friend. But now he just seemed to be a silly old fool of a pig. How could Tamworth behave like a pop-singing teenager over this little fat pig with nothing whatsoever to recommend her as far as Thomas could see?

Thomas had learnt that grown-ups almost always let you down at some time or another, but not Tamworth. Tamworth was different. All the glorious days, the happy adventures would be gone like a dandelion clock in a puff of wind if he were to start doting on some female. Furthermore, Thomas was convinced that if Tamworth had not been so enraptured by that same black and pink creature, the march would not have been ruined so easily by Deadly Dench and his gang, making fools of all of them.

They had been waiting for him at playtime, cat-calling and gloating, just as he knew they would be, Lurcher Dench and Christopher Robin Baggs and all their mates. Lurcher and Thomas had exchanged a blow each when scuds of rain swept violently across the playground and the whistle blew for them to come in. They had to be content with kicking each other in line, and being reprimanded for doing so.

At lunchtime the storm was so fierce that there was no chance at all of going outside, so they read and drew and played games in the classroom while, all around him, Thomas could hear the whispers.

"We'll get him. We'll finish him. Old Twopenny Tom! Old Measlebug. Tamworth Pig's a silly old fool, they ought to send him back to school. Measle-bug. Ugh! Chicken! Thomas is a lemon. Lame dog, Thomas. Chicken! Lame pig. Tamworth. Chicken! Chicken! Don't like it. Don't like it!"

He stuck his fingers in his ears and tried to read but there was no escape. He had no allies. He had gone to school late after a lot of illness, which was why he was known as Measlebug, and he did not make friends easily. He preferred animals. So he was alone against the class, though most of the girls probably would not interfere. Blossom and her friends would come to his aid if they could, but their classroom was on the far side of the school building and they would not be much use against Christopher Robin and his gang, plus Lurcher and his brothers, the school being full of Denches, all tough as old boots.

The afternoon break came after the puppet-making. The wind dropped at last and the clouds lifted for a moment. Play was outside even though the ground was wet with puddles. Thomas stuck his hands in his pockets, his head in the air and swaggered out on to the shiny asphalt. There they were, eleven of them, like a football line-up. They started to shuffle slowly to form a circle around him.

Thomas stood his ground as they approached and then leapt at Lurcher. If he could break him the rest would run. He grabbed the Dench locks and then jabbed to the chin with his left. But the others were now upon him. He managed to hit Christopher Robin right in his spotty face before he fell to the ground beneath a heap of thrusting, punching, hitting, kicking arms and legs. He did not see Henry, the Professor's son, brought up on strict methods of fair play, and horrified at such an unequal battle, rush forward to try to pull a few at least off the prostrate Thomas.

Then, from far away, sounded a fearsome ululation. Blossom's class emerged late from a reluctant Maths lesson, each moment of which was agony for Blossom answering everything wrong, and now, whooping and war-crying, they charged round the corner like young Amazons.

Encouraged, Thomas managed to squirm his way out of the scrum wriggling around and over him. But, by now, the many Dench brothers, Nosher, Basher,

Prodder and Crasher, had gathered their gangs from their assorted classes and were joyously hurtling into what looked like being the scrap of the year.

Minor battles broke out on the periphery of the main contest which heaved and surged like an enormous, many-tentacled monster in the middle of the playground.

There was little rhyme and less reason in the fighting. Boys hit their pals and girls kicked their best friends. Even the Infants, pouring in from their own playground, hopelessly pursued by a new and gentle helper, were screaming and pulling each other's hair and rolling on the wet ground.

Into the maelstrom strode Mrs. Twitchie, followed by the teacher on duty who had gone to fetch her. She blew her whistle. The heap of bodies disintegrated. Children picked themselves off the ground, then stood rooted to the spot. Mrs. Twitchie wasted no time.

"There will be no playtime tomorrow. The entire school will assemble in the hall and recite prayers instead."

Slowly she scanned the silent figures.

"Who began this fight?"

The finger of Gwendolyn Twitchie, the Headmistress's daughter, pointed at Thomas who stood wet, bruised and bleeding, sweater hanging like seaweed.

"Thomas, you will lose all next week's playtimes. You can come to me each day for a task to do."

He was past caring. All he wanted was a hole where he could hide away. But Blossom cried out in protest, and the measured voice of Henry spoke.

39

"I do not think that Thomas can be held entirely responsible."

Mrs. Twitchie was above minor interruptions. She waved a hand, the school crawled inside. Silence lay like a blanket save for one whisper.

"Wait till after school. We'll really get you then."

The rest of the afternoon was a blur to Thomas, but at last time for coats and caps and home came. He walked slowly out of the classroom towards the gate. No help there. All the parents waited at the Infant exit round the corner. Thomas walked out of the playground. Yes, there they were, twenty boys at least, perched up on the wall. Out of the corner of his eye, Thomas saw Henry move into step beside him. No

glasses, he thought. They must have been broken. The boys, led by Christopher Robin, jumped down from the wall. Thomas felt sick. He ached all over. Here we go again, he thought, lifting his grazed fists. That's odd. No Lurcher with them. Funny that. Still, makes it easier. Wait for it!

And through the air sounded the click of trotters and the ring of hoofs. Down the road came Tamworth, ears a-prick, tail curled up, every inch the pig of pigs, as a sudden gleam of watery sunshine struck the gold of his skin. Close behind him trotted Joe, the Shire Horse, and Barry MacKenzie Goat. Tamworth's eyes shone with all his old warmth and friendship. He surveyed the band of boys with amused contempt, then turned to Thomas.

"I thought you might be in need of a lift home today, dear boy. Jump up on my back."

Joe was rearing casually in the lane, showing his great hoofs, and Barry idly lowered his horns.

"Giddy-up, giddy-up, Tamworth," Thomas yelled, grinning all over his face.

What a glorious world! Being unhappy, being beaten was for other people! Nothing to do with him. He gripped the furry ears.

"Meet my friend. Here he is. He's called Henry. Tamworth, I've got a friend."

The waiting band of boys scattered in the face of such formidable opponents and slunk quietly away to their homes.

Chapter Five

---
*

"You see," Tamworth said to Blossom and Thomas as they sat in Pig House that evening, "I spent the whole day thinking and I came to the only possible conclusion."

"What's that?" Blossom asked.

"That I must never see Melanie again."

"Oh no!" Blossom cried.

"Very good idea. You don't really want to have anything to do with her, do you? Thomas asked.

"Yes," Tamworth replied.

They sat in silence for a moment.

"I don't hold with females, because they're always causing trouble," Hedgecock muttered. "I don't mean you, Blossom, but then you're not a proper female, are you?"

Blossom glared at him, mouth open with indignation, but Mr. Rab spoke up for her.

"I think Blossom is a delightful female," he said, and bowed a little bow.

"Shut up both of you," Thomas called out. "It doesn't matter whether she's a female or a washing machine. I want to know what Tamworth is going to do."

"I shall work even harder for the cause. I must save the trees. Melanie lives far away up north and will not come back here unless I ask her."

"Why did she come in the first place?" Thomas asked.

"She saw my photograph in the paper and persuaded the farmer's daughter to bring her to see me. But later I heard the farmer was angry with them, as it was a long journey. So that is that. Moreover, I have decided to devote my life to helping my country and domestic happiness has little part therein. Besides. . . ."

His voice quavered a little.

"She is a very young pig, too young for me."

"Oh, poor Tamworth," Blossom cried. "Never mind, you'll still have us."

"Yes, my dear, my very dear friends. We must think of her no more."

He shook himself a little and took a deep breath.

"Now, I want to plan the next march so that it is a real success. No more failures, eh, Thomas?"

Tamworth threw himself heart and soul into his campaign and the next march was splendidly attended. There were no motor bikes wrecking it this time because Tamworth obtained several tickets for a first division football match and contrived that Deadly Dench and his friends received them. He opened bazaars, held meetings and arranged sponsored walks. He spoke on the local television news and soon his campaign gained fame throughout the country. The Vicar's wife made a recording of "Save the Trees", and

it rose to number forty-three on the Top Fifty Records Chart, to the surprise of everyone except Mr. Rab, who thought it should have been number one.

Blossom and Thomas gathered great quantities of acorns, hazel and chestnuts and, every evening, they set off with nut-filled carrier bags to plant as many as possible in ditches, along hedgerows and on any available wasteland.

Thomas collected all the flower pots he could find and set orange and apple pips in them. He placed them in a dark cupboard along with the Christmas hyacinths planted by Mummy. In one of the pots, Mr. Rab planted a tinned strawberry.

"You stupid fool, that will never grow," Hedgecock snorted.

"Oh yes, it will. I've used a special compost for it. Think of all those beautiful tinned strawberries growing on trees."

Hedgecock rolled over and over, laughing so much that all his feathery prickles got tangled and he had to spend some time grooming himself.

Every day Mr. Rab inspected his little pot to see if the strawberry tree was coming up, but it never did. At last he dug up all the compost and looked for it but, of the strawberry, there was no sign at all.

He had a little weep to Blossom, when Hedgecock was not looking, because he did not want to look like the stripy fool Hedgecock always said he was.

"Never mind. Let's put a conker in a milk bottle with some water and watch it grow," Blossom consoled him.

Meanwhile the festivities of an English Autumn followed their traditional pattern. The Harvest Festival was followed by the Harvest Supper, a huge success, marred only for Thomas by the Vicar bending down from his lean and stately height to inquire how his conker collection was progressing. Thomas found himself incapable of speech. But the Vicar only smiled his austere smile and moved away to talk to someone else.

Hallowe'en was always well celebrated because October 31st was Blossom's birthday. This year she was to have a Fancy Dress party. She had a witch's cloak to wear with a tall hat and a broomstick, while Thomas had a black tracksuit with a luminous skeleton painted on it. Mr. Rab had a velvet coat, for he was to be the witch's cat, and Hedgecock a green toad. Masks were provided for one and all and black balloons with funny faces on them hung from the ceiling.

Thomas spent most of the day at Pig House, once he had inspected Blossom's presents to make sure she had not received something he especially wanted himself. (He was always jealous on Blossom's birthday.) However, only a beautiful set of felt pens aroused his envy, and she promised to lend them to him.

"I wish you'd come to the party, Tamworth," he said.

"I'll come along later to give her my present."

"I gave her a new poetry book," Mr. Rab said proudly.

"You give her one every year," Hedgecock snorted.

"She loves poetry. She liked it much better than your 'History of Numbers through the Ages'."

"I think it's marvellous."

"Maybe it is, to you, but you ought to buy people what they like, not what you like."

Hedgecock hit him hard. Mr. Rab sobbed and hugged himself with his thin paws.

"What a long day," Thomas yawned.

"That's because you're waiting for the party. What time does it begin?" Tamworth asked.

"Five o'clock, so that it will be dark for the games. I shall attack Gwendolyn Twitchie and make her horribly afraid."

He cheered up considerably at the beauty of this thought.

"Is she coming? I thought Blossom didn't like her any more," Tamworth said.

"She wasn't invited at first, but she kicked up such a fuss that Blossom asked her after all. I wouldn't have done."

Five o'clock at last arrived and so did the guests, strangely clean and subdued, clutching parcels. Daddy went out muttering about some important business he had to see to. Mrs. Postlewaithe had come to help Mummy with the food. Jolly good it was too, baked chestnuts and baked potatoes, hot doughnuts and spiced buns, as well as the usual jelly, ice-cream, crisps and lemonade. Lights were turned off, and

49

candles lit in the pumpkins as the guests approached the food, politely at first.

Ten minutes later they looked more their usual selves, with hair and hats falling down, costumes drenched in lemonade or Coca-Cola, and Mrs. Postlewaithe on her hands and knees on the floor picking up abandoned buns and sandwiches.

Birthday cake was to come later, so masks were donned to play the first game, Pass the Parcel. Despite wild cheating and snatching by Thomas, it was won by Gwendolyn Twitchie. Thomas retired to a corner to brood on his revenge. Musical Bumps and Dead Lions followed. Gwendolyn won Dead Lions too.

Seeing Thomas's angry scowls, Mummy decided it would be a good idea to have the moonlight walk in the garden before the fancy dresses fell apart. The children were very excited by this and ran up and down the garden path whooping and playing ghosts. At last, Mrs. Postlewaithe blew a whistle and counted the heads as they came in again.

"It's all right," she said. "Eighteen heads altogether."

"Your Thomas seems to be enjoying himself," she went on, while the children scattered for hide and seek. "He was smiling all over his face."

Mummy was just putting out the birthday cake. She looked surprised.

"That's odd. He usually hates parties, especially girls' parties."

Blossom knew a splendid hiding-place, behind the blankets in the airing cupboard. She wriggled in happily and thought what a wonderful day she was

having. A figure crept in beside her. Oh bother, it's Thomas, she thought. She peered in the gloom. It did not seem like Thomas. As far as she could see it was not anyone she knew at all. She started to tremble and edged forward to push the door open. Light streamed in.

"What's up?" asked the figure.

She knew that voice. Relief made her furious. She stopped trembling.

"Lurcher Dench!" she snapped crossly and pulled off his mask.

"Ow!" he exclaimed as the sharp elastic bit him.

"What are you doing here? I didn't invite you."

"I know. I'm sorry."

Blossom stared at the old enemy. Grey eyes looked pleadingly out of a freckled face.

"You see, I never go to parties. Nobody ever asks me, and Mum never 'as a party. Not with all us lads."

Blossom tried to go on looking angry.

"I like you, Blossom. I like the stories you tell. I'd like you to tell me some, and please, can I stop and 'ave some cake?"

A slow grin spread across her face.

"When did you get in?"

"With the kids in the garden. I made me costume. Look, it's newspaper and I painted it black and joined the rest."

"That's funny. I thought Mum counted us, and Mrs. Postlewaithe definitely did. She must have got it wrong. Come on, let's give up. I want to see Thomas's face when he sees you."

Thomas won the game of Hide and Seek, hidden under a sack of potatoes in the pantry. He came out to receive his prize and saw Lurcher. Stiff with rage he stalked over to him.

"Outside," he hissed, jerking his thumb.

"Don't go. I'm just going to blow out the candles and cut the cake," Blossom cried, but they completely ignored her as they marched to the door in their newspaper and skeleton outfits.

Mummy came in from the kitchen.

"Come on, Blossom. What are you waiting for?"

She hesitated for a moment, then blew out the candles. Whatever happened, food was always a great comfort.

Thomas and Lurcher took up their positions on the lawn and fought long and silently in the dark and the cold, oblivious of the singing and laughter inside. They were alone for the first time, their battle uncomplicated by interfering adults, allies or spectators, the issue straightforward at last, Thomas or Lurcher.

They were well matched, Lurcher the heavier, Thomas faster. Lurcher stronger but Thomas fiercer. They struck and danced away, weaving, dodging and punching in the moonlight. Thomas fought for his own territory and Lurcher fought for the right to enter Blossom's world of stories, games and campaigns.

At last they broke and fell back, battered, exhausted but satisfied, all hatred gone, the result a draw. The lawn was littered with the shreds of the newspaper costume.

They entered the room arm in arm and advanced for their share of the cake. Parents were arriving to take away the guests. Mummy was handing each one a lollipop when her eyes alighted on the battle-marked pair. Swiftly she pushed them into the kitchen.

"I'll deal with you later," she said grimly.

They sat with quiet resignation awaiting her return. After a while, Thomas found a cold flannel for his bleeding mouth and handed Lurcher a dishcloth for his swollen eye. They listened to the noise of those departing. This noise crescendoed enormously.

"That sounds like Mrs. Twitchie," Lurcher remarked.

Thomas tried to grin despite his painful lips.

"I'd forgotten," he said.

"Forgotten what?"

"I locked Gwendolyn in the shed when we went round the garden and I forgot to let her out."

"That's why Ma Postlewaithe didn't spot me when she counted us in."

Voices and footsteps came near. Angry voices, hard steps. United they turned to meet their doom.

But later, when all the telling off was over and Mrs. Twitchie and Gwendolyn had finally gone, Blossom was waiting with two vast slices of cake and lollipops for all the Dench children.

Chapter Six

Half-term arrived and, on one fine afternoon,
Blossom, Thomas, Tamworth, Hedgecock and Mr.
Rab set off for the Tumbling Wood. Mr. Rab's nose
was a-twitch with excitement at the prospect of
visiting the Welsh Rabbit once more.

Thomas carried a bag to collect sweet chestnuts,
this time, for the year's crop was a record one and they
lay on the ground in thousands just waiting to be
picked up. Never had there been such a time for nuts.
The squirrels had filled every nest and every secret
cache and still the woods were carpeted with them.

Sweet chestnut cases are very prickly, and hands and
paws grew sore as they picked up one after another,
cracking the outer shells to reveal the brown nuts
curled inside, three of them, unlike the single conker.

At last, the bag full, they stopped, content. Six
hundred and thirty-one nuts Hedgecock reported, a
pleasant addition to the food Tamworth and Blossom
had brought with them. They both believed that food
improved all occasions.

They left Mr. Rab by the elderberry bush so that he
could see his friend, then rambled on to the centre of
the wood.

"Let's eat something, I'm starving," Blossom said.

"Wait until we find the right place," Thomas answered.

"How do we know when it is the right place?"

"I shall know when I see it," he said, running along the path with Hedgecock. Tamworth and Blossom followed more slowly, thinking about food.

Suddenly he turned sharply right, straight up the wooded hill.

"There's a path here. Come on!" he called.

"I cannot perceive any sign whatsoever of a path, dear boy," Tamworth puffed.

"Nor me," Blossom agreed.

This was not surprising, as she was quietly investigating the picnic bag to see if she could sneak a chocolate biscuit without anyone noticing.

"I think I got the number right," Hedgecock was muttering to himself. "I think it was six hundred and thirty-one, not six hundred and twenty-three."

Thomas ran ahead up the slope, brushing aside nettles and brambles.

"Look, somebody's cut steps here."

Between the moss and the fallen leaves, the edge of a stone step showed. On and up they climbed, Thomas now far ahead, almost seeming to fly. The others stumbled after, scratched and nettled and not at all eager.

At last Thomas stopped and the others caught up with him. A great ring of giant beech trees loomed up against the sky at the summit of the hill. Within this ring stretched a smooth, green lawn, all soft, springy

grass, clear of nettles or bracken. Right in the centre
stood a tree of immense girth, the widest tree they had
ever seen, with powerful branches growing almost

57

horizontally from the trunk. They ran to it and tried to encircle it, but they could not.

"It makes you look small, Tamworth," Thomas shouted.

"It's a British Oak, the finest tree in the world. It takes three hundred years to grow, three hundred years to live, three hundred years to die and a hundred years to fall down."

"That's a thousand years," Hedgecock breathed in delight.

"Oh, do let's eat here. I love this place. Mr. Rab would say that it was enchanted," Blossom exclaimed.

"Silly old fool. I'm glad he isn't here or he'd be going on about fairies," Hedgecock replied.

They laid an old groundsheet on the short turf and sat down. Soon all was silent save for the sound of eating. At the bottom of the bag, Thomas found a paper flag left over from summer days. He put it in his pocket, climbed on to Tamworth's back and managed to haul himself on to the lowest branch. There he fixed his flag, a Union Jack.

"My tree," he remarked as he descended.

"Our tree," Blossom corrected him.

"The tree of Saint Thomas."

Blossom did not bother to reply. Sometimes it just was not worth arguing with Thomas. But she thought to herself that it would always be the king of the wood for her.

At last they decided to go home, turning at the ring of beech trees for one last look at the noble oak. They could just see Thomas's little flag.

"You know, that tree might have been growing when William the Conqueror invaded the land," Tamworth said.

He looked thoughtful.

"For me, it seems to stand for all the trees in the country."

Mr. Rab was waiting for them beside the elderberry bush. He was very excited and would not listen when they tried to tell him about the oak tree. He was full of his own news.

"My friend the Welsh Rabbit says there's trouble coming to this wood. All the wild animals are full of strange rumours. More and more machines are arriving and men in bowler hats pop up everywhere."

"We haven't seen any machines today," Tamworth said.

"There are six on the other side of the wood, he says."

Tamworth looked grave.

"I have a feeling the wood is in danger. It is going to need our campaign."

Chapter Seven

*

Late that night the wind rose and howled loudly. Towards dawn it reached an absolute pitch of fury, shrieking and whistling wildly. People awoke and got up, unable to sleep again as tiles and slates flew off roofs, garage doors banged and blew in, dustbin lids clashed and clanged in back yards, and fences collapsed like broken matchboxes.

The cricket pavilion was lifted over the hedge and whirled into the pond of the next field. Two of the Vicarage chimney pots were toppled off. Lights were switched on one by one, then went off simultaneously as a line was blown down and the power failed.

Mr. Baggs went round his farm to see that all the animals were safe. Last of all he called into Pig House to visit Tamworth, who was wide awake, staring out of his window at the wild storm-tossed world outside.

"The wind's not doing your trees any good, Tamworth. Branches are falling everywhere. There'll be a lot of damage by morning."

Tamworth turned to Farmer Baggs and sighed.

"It's a sad sight, a sad sight."

"You all right, then, Tamworth?"

"Oh yes. I'm all right. Thank you for calling to see me."

He turned back to the window.

"Lost a bit of weight, 'ee 'ave, Tamworth," Farmer Baggs said, eyeing him.

"Yes, I have. I am somewhat smaller round my middle, I regret to say."

"I'll send 'ee a fresh lot of cabbages, tomorrow. We can't 'ave 'ee getting thin. 'T would never do."

"Thank you, kind friend. I do seem to have lost my appetite lately."

"Well, we'll soon back 'ee up. Try and get some sleep, now, mind. Goodnight, Tamworth."

"Goodnight, Farmer Baggs."

The farmer closed the door behind him and the wind blew louder than ever.

"Summat's wrong with that pig," he muttered to himself as he staggered back to the house, buffeted and beaten by wayward gusts, blowing from all directions.

In his bed, Thomas wrapped Num carefully around Hedgecock and Mr. Rab. They had all been awake for a long time. Mr. Rab trembled pitifully as he listened to the ferocious roar.

"I keep imagining that raggetty men pretending to be leaves are dancing with the wind," he wailed. "They've got mean, pointed faces and they're coming to fetch me, to take me into the cold, dark night and I'm afraid."

He hid his nose, pale with terror, in Num's soft folds.

"Raggetty stuffed vegetables! All we have to worry about is if the roof blows off," Hedgecock snapped.

Mr. Rab wailed again.

"I do hope my friend the Welsh Rabbit is safe. Fancy being in a wood on a night like this."

"Oh, he's all right. They're used to roughing it out there. Come on, let's recite a few multiplication tables to cheer ourselves up. There's nothing like the seven times to give one a bit of comfort."

Once more Mr. Rab wailed.

"Oh no, I can't think of anything less comfortable than the seven times table except the eighth or the ninth."

But Thomas also thought tables a good idea and he and Hedgecock had reached eleven times nine is ninety-nine when Mummy opened the door, bearing a candle in an old brass candlestick. She straightened the bed and tucked them all in.

"I'll leave the candle on the chest. It's quite safe and it's a pretty light. I think the wind will die down soon."

At that moment, the most tremendous noise of all was heard, like ten trains crashing. Every window in the house rattled and Mr. Rab shot right down the bed to Thomas's feet in terror.

"What was that?" Blossom cried, rushing in.

She had slept soundly up to then, to be awoken by this most monstrous of sounds.

"I don't know," Mummy said.

Daddy loomed large in the doorway.

"I think it's the elm tree in the village fallen at last. I thought it would, one day. Elm trees have shallow roots and often fall in gales. One tree you couldn't save, Thomas."

"Now off to sleep, everyone. I'm pretty sure the worst is over," Mummy added.

Everyone went to see the tree the next day. It had fallen at an angle down the road, and fortunately no houses were damaged. It looked defenceless with its roots snatched out of the ground.

"Poor tree," Blossom said.

Later, with the branches lopped off and the trunk sawn up, it made a huge bonfire for Guy Fawkes Night. Blossom and Thomas were not very keen on November the Fifth, because all their animal friends hated it so. However, this year, they went to watch

the tree burn in a tremendous fire in a field loaned by
Farmer Baggs.

At school, pictures were painted and poems written

65

about the fire. Blossom's picture, all black and scarlet and yellow, went up on the wall. Thomas's poem was read out to his class.

> "*Tree growing to the sky,*
> *Flames flowing to the sky,*
> *So did it live,*
> *So did it die.*"

"Very good," commented Mr. Starling, their teacher, who was keen on poetry.

Thomas did not tell him that Mr. Rab had made it up in bed the night before the bonfire.

Lurcher Dench's work was read out too, for the first time ever.

> "*I like to see the big bonfire*
> *I like to see the rockets.*
> *Mrs. Twitchie says we mustn't*
> *Have bangers in our pockets.*"

Blossom heard all the Denches read in the dinner-hour now. Led by a determined Lurcher, they would appear with their reading books. After she had listened to them read, she would tell them one of her own stories. They listened to every word, the Denches now being as fiercely keen on reading as on fighting.

A strange quiet hung over the school, in fact. Christopher Robin, spotty as ever, walked around with Gwendolyn Twitchie. Only occasionally did Thomas, peacefully racing cars with his friend Henry, regret the old warfare, the joy of battle.

"We're getting soppy," he complained to Tamworth.

"And a good thing too, dear boy. Violence is always to be deplored."

"What's deplored?" Thomas asked.

"I deplore Hedgecock," Mr. Rab said.

"Not half as much as I deplore you," Hedgecock snarled, kicking him hard.

Chapter Eight

*

A Jumble Sale was to be held in the School Hall for the Save the Trees campaign funds. Tamworth was going to be there so that people could guess his weight, and a huge cake was the prize for the most accurate estimate. Blossom had promised to help Mummy at a stall, selling old coats, hats and suits.

Thomas went with them most reluctantly. He loathed Jumble Sales, hating everything about them, the smell of old clothes, the frantic rush bearing down on the stalls when the doors opened, the Vicar speaking to him, and Mummy and Blossom gossiping to people he could hardly bear to be in the same room with.

A boy in Blossom's class was disposing of his Matchbox series of cars, so he bought as many of these as he could afford, then mooched around the hall, hands stuffed in pockets, face scowling. He purchased a toffee apple, but could not finish it, so he threw it away behind the piano, and looked up to find the Vicar towering over him. He picked it up hastily, contemplated the dust it had now acquired and walked round trying to find a place to dump it.

"Humph. Fancy, with all this rotten old rubbish everywhere, you can't even get rid of a toffee apple," he muttered.

Finally, he dropped it in his mother's shopping basket. She looked up.

"Thomas, please stay and help at this stall for a moment. I simply must speak to the Vicar's wife. I shan't be long."

"What do I do?" he asked desperately.

"Just take the money they give you for the clothes and put it in this tin. Blossom will help you with the change."

"I can do it better than she can, the stupid, fat nit."

"All right, then. I'll only be a moment. Oh, and do watch your language, Thomas.. People don't always like your rude way of talking."

"I shan't speak at all then," he grumbled.

He noticed, crossly, that Mrs. Twitchie and Gwendolyn were selling cakes at the next stall.

"Bet that lot are poisonous," he thought aloud.

People came to the stall, picked up garments and handed him money. He put it in the tin. It grew very hot, so he took off his anorak. Mummy seemed to be gone a long time, but he was doing quite well. One or two people were obviously pleased with their bargains. He was getting into the swing of it when Mummy appeared.

"Thank you, Thomas. I'm sorry I was so long."

"I did very well. I got fifty pence for one coat. Can I go now?"

"Yes. Tell Daddy I'll be coming soon."

He had almost reached the door, encountering a crowd of new arrivals, when a clear voice rang out.

"That woman is wearing my coat!"

It was a voice accustomed to command, the voice of Mrs. Twitchie. Thomas watched her run across the hall and seize the arm of a large woman wearing a blue sheepskin coat. It looked familiar, somehow.

"I've just bought it," came the equally loud voice of Mrs. Dench, also accustomed to instant obedience.

All the fighting Denches took after her, not Dad, who was small and silent, and never worked.

"You can't have done. It's not for sale. I only took it off for a moment. Give it to me."

"Yes, it was. I gave fifty pence for it. That's a lot at a Jumble Sale, but it's a good coat."

"Of course it is. I gave fifty pounds for it," Mrs. Twitchie cried.

People began to gather round. This was very interesting. Then Thomas remembered suddenly and clearly. His bargain! He'd sold the coat to Mrs. Dench. He tried to edge his way through the throng to escape outside.

"I bought it from the stall. I paid for it and I'm keeping it."

By now the Denches had all gathered round their Mum. She drew herself up to her full height, looming over Mrs. Twitchie, who was going red down her neck with fury. She leaned forward and started to undo the buttons, which only just fastened anyway. Mrs. Dench pulled the edges together again.

"And that's my duffle," Gwendolyn shrieked, pointing at Lurcher, who certainly looked smarter than usual.

The Vicar and his wife now came forward.

"I'm sure we can solve this problem. Is this Mrs. Twitchie's coat, my dear?"

"Yes, I think so."

"Of course it is," Mrs. Twitchie bellowed.

She was not used to having her word doubted. The Vicar patted her arm. She pushed him off.

"You've got to do something," she snapped.

"Mrs. Dench, you must see that this is all a mistake. We'll gladly refund the money. Which stall was it?"

The Vicar was trying hard to keep the peace.

"Mrs. Thingummy's," Mrs. Dench said, pointing

at Mummy's stall. "That small boy Timothy sold it to me."

She could never remember her own children's names, let alone anyone else's.

Silence fell as heads turned to the stall, then searched round the hall for Thomas. Frantically he tried to push his way out. Mummy had gone very pink.

"I'm sorry. I shouldn't have left Thomas here. He must have sold it."

Blossom, weeping, flung her arms round her.

"It's not my Mummy's fault," she cried.

"We all know whose fault it is. Thomas, come here!"

Mrs. Twitchie's stentorian tones filled the hall.

Thomas turned blindly, hemmed in by people, who stared at him, pushing him forward. He could not get his breath. Panic rose in him. All these horrible people! And he had not meant it. It was not fair, she must have left her coat near the stall. He had only tried to help.

Something soft thrust into his hand. It was Tamworth's snout. The crowd fell back at last as the huge pig moved to his friend.

"Up, Thomas. Get on my back, old lad."

He pulled himself on to the familiar, golden back as the deep voice rang out, drowning the angry splutters of Mrs. Dench and Mrs. Twitchie.

"Friends," Tamworth cried, "let us not make fools of ourselves. Let us be calm and sensible. Thomas, my dear friend here, made a mistake. Well, which of us has never made a mistake? We all have made mistakes. And, by the way, that's Thomas's anorak you're wearing, Crasher Dench. You see, Mrs. Twitchie, Thomas was quite fair. He sold his own clothes, too."

The crowd laughed. The Vicar smiled his austere smile.

"Come, Mrs. Dench. Give Mrs. Twitchie her coat. Your money and our apologies shall be given to you."

The clothes were handed back, the money returned.

"Furthermore," Tamworth said blandly, his voice like cream, "Mrs. Dench has guessed my weight correctly and so has won the cake, which, I'm sure, will be appreciated by her admirable family."

Mrs. Dench looked astonished, as well she might, never having bought a ticket to guess Tamworth's weight. Then she smiled.

"Thank you, Tamworth."

"Thank you, madam. And thank you, Mrs. Twitchie, for your kind forgiveness of us all."

Mrs. Twitchie was still glowering alternately at Thomas and the Denches.

Never one to lose an opportunity, Tamworth concluded, "Thank you, everyone. Remember our cause, and come to the next march. Save the trees!"

"Save the trees!" re-echoed through the hall. The Vicar's wife began to sing.

"Shush, my dear," the Vicar said.

She stopped singing.

Mummy went up to Mrs. Dench and said quietly, "Let Crasher keep the anorak. I think he likes it."

The entertainment was over, so the crowd moved on. Thomas stroked Tamworth's ears and slid off his back. Lurcher Dench pulled his arm, his eyes like slits.

"We don't want your manky old clothes."

They glared at one another and together pushed their way outside to the field behind the hall.

Lurcher kicked Thomas's shin. Thomas punched him on his nose.

"That's better," he panted almost happily, as they fell to the ground pummelling each other.

Life was back to normal again. Tamworth would disapprove, Mummy would grumble, but Thomas knew that when he and Lurcher were fighting each other, everything was all right.

Chapter Nine

———————————— * ————————————

At first Tamworth would not believe the news, then, gradually, he realized that it must be true. He looked at the two small forms, both hanging on his words, expecting him to think of the solution to their problems, then and there.

"You say that the motorway is going to by-pass the village, which we knew, but that, instead of going east through the slag heaps, where we thought it would go, and where it would only improve the landscape, it is being directed straight through Tumbling Wood, so that the hill will be levelled and all the wood destroyed. Is that it, my friend?"

"Yes, indeed to goodness," the Welsh Rabbit replied. "From all directions reports are coming in, they are, man."

He lowered his voice.

"Some do say that the Minister of Environment has been all over the woods, himself in person."

"We've met Ministers before," Mr. Rab quavered. "They're nothing to Tamworth."

He tried to snap his paws but failed lamentably. He was very nervous. Tamworth perceived that he had described his friends to the Welsh Rabbit as being very clever and important and he was anxious that they should live up to this. But the Welsh Rabbit did not look as if he were easily impressed.

"Mr. Rab, my friend here, said that you got things done, that you had influence, man. That's why the animals in the wood sent me to see you, to stop this terrible thing, this threat to our lives and our homes."

Tamworth looked grave.

"I don't think that I've the sort of influence that moves motorways. Besides, I like motorways. I think they will solve traffic problems and bring prosperity, but that we must be sure they take the best path through the countryside."

He sat back on his haunches and brooded for a while. Mr. Rab twitched and wriggled, but managed to keep silent for once. At last Tamworth spoke.

"I think this is all we can do. First, write to the Minister and find out definitely if the motorway is to go through the wood. Second, if so, we must get up a petition asking if the original route can be used instead. Third, promote publicity about the wood and its beauty. It's not very well known at present. Fourth, carry on with our 'Save the Trees' campaign."

He reflected for a moment.

"Plans have been changed, though not often. Let us hope, my friends, that this will be one of those rare successes."

"Thank you, Tamworth the Pig. I see what they are saying, you are indeed a clever pig, and we shall in your trotters leave it. I will tell the wood dwellers that you are trying to save them. Or else at the worst it is, we have all lost our homes."

"Indeed to goodness, yes," Mr. Rab agreed.

So began the biggest campaign ever. Blossom and Thomas drew poster after poster. Tamworth, getting steadily thinner, held meetings and toured the country-side on Farmer Baggs's tractor, speaking through a loud hailer. He went into school and addressed the children. Mrs. Twitchie was most polite, for Tam-worth as a Very Important Pig was quite different from Tamworth, friend of terrible Thomas.

Next day the children were all gathered together in the school garden. Mrs. Twitchie, wearing a mackin-tosh and gumboots, emerged with Mr. Starling follow-ing. He carried a small sapling and a spade. Mrs Twitchie's clarion tones rang out.

"Children! I am about to plant a tree!"

She took the spade from Mr. Starling and dug into the ground. There was a clink as it struck a stone.

Thomas watched with mixed feelings. He wanted to save trees, especially the Tumbling Wood trees, very much indeed, but he hated being on the same side as Mrs. Twitchie. He started to wriggle. He wanted to kick Christopher Robin Baggs, standing just in front of him, but Blossom slid in quietly beside him. She knew how he felt.

"Tamworth says we have to use all the support we can get when it's a Cause, even if it's someone we don't like," she whispered.

So Thomas stood still, while Mrs. Twitchie, tired of

digging, handed over the spade for Mr. Starling to finish the job. A cheer went up as the tree was finally planted. Thomas tried to join in but he could not, and was saved by a gusty shower of rain splattering over them, speeding them all back to the classrooms.

Meanwhile the Vicar's wife knitted sweaters with "Save the Trees" on the front. These proved popular

and soon all the children were wearing them. Lurcher Dench liked his very much. He had not had a new sweater for ages. A famous firm got to hear of them and bought the pattern from her for a large sum of money, and hundreds of sweaters were made in their factories. With this and the money from her record, she became quite rich. However, the Vicar did not like this at all and made her give most of the money away to charity. She did buy a beautiful red velvet dress, though. Mummy went with her to choose it.

Tamworth wrote to a badge manufacturer and soon thousands of green and gold "Save the Trees" badges were being worn on tee-shirts throughout the length and breadth of the land, as their owners went out to plant nuts, pips and seeds in all sorts of likely and unlikely places from quiet lanes to cracks and crevices in concrete yards.

Tamworth was asked to appear on "This Week in England", a television programme.

Thomas brushed him and scratched his back.

"Shall I shampoo you like I did before, when you went on television?"

"No, not that again," Tamworth said, shuddering at the memory of it. "The water was icy."

"I know," Thomas said, and shot away to return with a large tin of talcum powder which he up-ended over Tamworth.

"Atishoo! Atishoo!" Tamworth trumpeted, now a white not a golden pig.

He looked at himself in the Pig House mirror and groaned.

"I look like the ghost of a pig."

But Thomas brushed so firmly and steadily that Tamworth's coat emerged, shining and clean, though a slightly paler shade of gold.

"That's better. By the time the make-up girls have finished with me, I shan't look too bad."

Suddenly he looked sad.

"But I am not the Pig I was, you know, Thomas, I'm much too thin."

"You're all right. I know, smoke your new pipe in between questions. It will give you the right air."

Tamworth's television appearance went off well and the number of visitors to the Tumbling Wood increased tenfold.

"Beauty Spot In Danger—Pig Speaks" ran the headline in a famous daily newspaper.

But one evening, when Blossom was returning home from a music lesson, she found Joe the Shire Horse waiting for her.

"I want a word with 'ee, Blossom," he said in his slow way.

"Yes, Joe. What's it all about?"

She felt in her anorak pocket for a lump of sugar. She found two, and they both crunched together.

"It be about Tamworth."

"What about him?"

"Well, 'ee don't laugh no more and 'ee don't sleep. Night after night 'ee's up and down Pig 'ouse."

"He's very busy saving the trees."

"It ain't only that. He sits dreaming for hours, reciting bits o' poetry."

"He's always recited poetry."

"Not love poetry! And worst of all, 'ee's getting so thin."

"Yes, lots of people have noticed. They keep writing to him, asking if he's on a diet and can he recommend one. But Tamworth doesn't want to be thin. Well, Joe, what do you think is wrong?"

Joe bent his head low and whispered in her ear. She nodded.

"Yes, yes. I'll see to it. I really will. I'll do all I can, Joe, I promise."

So Blossom went home to make inquiries and to write letters that had nothing whatsoever to do with saving trees or moving motorways.

Chapter Ten

*

Daddy piled a great deal of marmalade on to his toast and reached out for the Sunday papers with a sigh of satisfaction. He turned to the sports page, then fixed an irritable eye on Blossom.

"What are you tittering about?"

"You dropped a chunk of marmalade in your tea."

He arose, stalked to the kitchen, tipped the tea down the sink, returned and poured out another cup, then sat down and reached for his newspaper, holding it up firmly between Blossom and himself. A minute passed peacefully.

"Daddy," she cried.

"Oh! For heaven's sake, what's the matter now?"

"Look at that."

"At what? England's doing well in Australia."

"No, no. Look at this page. Here."

"I wish you wouldn't read the paper when I do."

"But look, please."

"What at?"

" 'Mrs. Baggs Speaks. Exclusive Interview. Pig is wrong, she says.' "

Daddy found the place and continued aloud.

" 'In an interview with our reporter, Mrs. Baggs stroked her curls' . . ."

"What, those greasy sausages?" Thomas interrupted.

" 'and talked to us in her beautiful farmhouse.' "

"You mean that smelly old dump."

" ' "Tamworth Pig is a threat to our country," she said. "He hinders progress and ruins the morals of the young" ' . . ."

"What's morals?" Thomas asked.

"Goodness and things. Oh, never mind. Let me go on. ' "He's big-headed and pig-headed," ' she continued, looking every inch a farmer's wife' . . ."

"And there's hundreds of inches of her," Thomas shouted.

" . . . ' "I have treated that pig like my own child, and I have received nothing but ingratitude and unkind words. I fed him with my own hands and the finest food" ' . . ."

"I hope she kept them separate," Mummy put in.

" . . . ' "and so he started his Grow More Food campaign and spoke against me" ' . . ."

"Oh, how can she tell such lies?" Blossom breathed.

" . . . ' "Mrs. Baggs, what do you think of his latest campaign to save Tumbling Wood," our reporter asked. "It's a shame and a disgrace. The wood is an eyesore, full of rotting trees and rubbish that has been dumped there" ' . . ."

"If there's any rubbish, she must have put it there. I bet she would too, the old ratbag."

"Thomas!" Mummy said in a horrified voice.

Daddy lowered the paper.

"Loyalty to your friends should not affect your language, Thomas. By the way, I think Mrs. Baggs's brother Bert is a sub-contractor to the firm building the motorway, which may account for her attitude."

He read on.

"'Our reporter then said that he believed that Farmer Baggs was very fond of Tamworth Pig. "He's a gentle, kind man, Mr. Baggs is, and he cannot see the villainy that is in such a wicked animal as that pig, but, in time, we shall all see," she concluded.'"

Thomas was drumming with his heels, his face bright crimson.

"I'm going to kill her," he said.

"You mustn't talk like that, Thomas. It does no good," Mummy reproved him.

"I'm off to take it to Tamworth," Thomas said.

"Tamworth has all the Sunday newspapers anyway, so he won't need this one. Don't worry about him, he'll know what to do," Daddy replied.

In fact, Tamworth treated the whole thing as a joke and was especially polite to Mrs. Baggs when she appeared with his food as usual, a smirk in the corners of her mouth.

But Thomas spent the day in a state of fury, planning revenges, none of which seemed likely to succeed. It was no use kidnapping her or emptying Tamworth's food over her head. He did think of putting on his skeleton costume and hiding in her wardrobe so that he could jump out at her when she had gone to bed, but it really did not seem practicable.

What he did do, in the end, was to waylay Christopher Robin Baggs, seize him by his bow tie, force him

down on his knees, and compel him to say that Tamworth Pig was the greatest.

Christopher Robin squirmed and tears ran down his cheeks, but afterwards he told Mrs. Twitchie about it, so Thomas came off worse after all. He was barred from football until the end of term because of his lack of sportsmanship.

After school, he sat bitterly beside Tamworth under the damson tree.

"It's not fair," he said.

"I told you violence is wrong," Tamworth murmured to him, rubbing his snout against him. "We must be patient and bide our time, Thomas."

"I don't like patience and biding. I like fighting and winning," Thomas said with great conviction.

Chapter Eleven

*

It was the Welsh Rabbit, on swiftly flying paws, who brought the news to Mr. Rab.

"The campaign has failed. Bulldozers have up the wood started to tear."

Blossom and Thomas rushed to Tamworth and five minutes later he was riding through the village on Farmer Baggs's tractor, calling through a loud-speaker to a rapidly gathering audience.

"Brothers! Friends! A cry for help has sounded. We must help our brothers the trees and those who live in their shelter. Without warning, the machines are moving in to destroy the prettiest spot in the whole country. Come, let us to the wood. Let us save the trees!"

A ragged cheer arose. Tamworth held up a trotter.

"Forward, my friends. To the wood!"

Children rushed away, to return with flags and banners, and set off behind Tamworth, Blossom and Thomas. Hedgecock and Mr. Rab climbed up on Joe's back. The students appeared, being ever on the alert for a demonstration, and animals and birds came running and flying. Rather more slowly, the grown-ups joined in the procession, one at a time, at first, then in twos and threes until they were pouring out of their houses, rallied by the Vicar's wife's voice ringing through the air.

> "*Save the Trees,*
> *Save the Trees,*
> *We're marching over there to save the trees!*"

Lurcher ran up beside Joe.

"We're with you on this," he shouted to the unwelcoming face of Thomas who had climbed on Joe's back. "Deadly's coming to help, too."

"You'd better," Thomas snarled, then lent a hand to haul him up.

The roar of motor bikes was heard as the leatherjackets formed an escort to the procession.

P.C. Cubbins and P.C. Spriggs ran out, but they could only go along with the steadily increasing throng.

"Forward!" Tamworth cried. "It is the Cause!"

More and more people joined in. Cars and Land-Rovers bumped along the track as folks from outlying farms and houses enrolled.

> "*Save the Trees,*
> *Save the Trees.*"

The cry seemed to rise up to the sky.

"Tamworth," Thomas shouted. "Tam—worth. Tam—worth."

"Tam—worth. Tam—worth. Tam—worth," took up the crowd.

Blossom felt wild excitement rising within her. She

felt like flying, like crying. This was living. This was life. This was better than anything that had ever happened. This was the way to the stars. People were wonderful. People could do anything, save anything. She felt proud. She felt she had wings, a crown on her head, a fire in her heart. She looked at Thomas and Lurcher, loving them. And their eyes were bright and wild, their faces red. She looked at everyone around and behind her, and saw flushed, singing faces, with no sense in any of them. The excitement left her and Blossom was afraid.

"Joe, Joe," she cried in his ear. "Let me down. Let me down. I must see Tamworth."

He paused a moment and she slid off. The crowd pressed up behind and she felt terrified. Now there was no stopping, only going on. Somehow she got up to the tractor.

"Tamworth," she called.

The tractor slowed down and she climbed on to it.

"Tamworth! Oh, Tamworth. I don't like it. They're all mad. Someone will get hurt."

She pulled at him. She wanted to see his face. He turned to her. Tamworth's eyes were as kind and calm as Mummy's were when she told bedtime stories.

"Don't let them . . ." she started.

"It's all right, dear Blossom. No one will get hurt. There will be no violence."

"Are you sure?"

"I promise," said Tamworth Pig.

The wood came into sight.

"There they are," the crowd roared. "The machines.

There are the machines. Wreck them! Wreck them!"

Blossom looked at the earth-movers and shuddered.

"Oh, Tamworth. What are we doing?" she whispered.

The crowd was moving rapidly now, shouting, calling, singing, booing. "Save the trees! Wreck the machines!"

"Stop," Tamworth called.

The crowd stopped. Cars and bikes braked erratically. There was a terrible roar like a tide surging on a storm-ridden beach.

"Quiet," Tamworth said.

There was silence. Tamworth spoke, his voice gentle as a summer breeze.

"Brothers and friends. We are here to save, not to destroy, to conserve, not to ruin. We come with love, not hate. Let there be no talk of wrecking. I will speak to the men of the machines."

He drove the tractor forward to the foremost bulldozer. The driver was dark and angry.

"Get those lunatics out of here. We've got a job to do. Out of the way!"

Tamworth held up a trotter.

"I would not stop any man doing his job. I only ask you to wait for a time. I think the plans may be altered, so please don't destroy this wood."

The dark, angry one glowered.

"Get that lot out of here. Come on, men!"

The machines turned towards the wood.

Tamworth's voice boomed like a jet plane.

"Save the trees!"

Like a huge cloud settling on a mountain top, people and animals surged forward and lay down in the path of the bulldozers. They wrapped themselves round the trees and stayed there. Blossom caught sight of the Vicar's wife lowering her long form to curl round a beech tree and Mr. Rab scurrying away to the elderberry bush. Thomas climbed up beside her. The motor bikes lay scattered on the ground.

"We are prepared to stay here day and night," Tamworth announced calmly.

"Till nine o' clock anyway. I got a date wiv a bird, then," Deadly yelled.

A ginger-haired man dropped down from his earth-mover.

"I'm off home," he said. "I haven't had a Saturday off in weeks. Best of luck, folks. It's a nice wood."

The others followed suit, till only the dark, angry one remained. At last he spoke.

"I'll go. But I'll have you for this, pig!"

The crowd got up slowly to return home to television and Saturday tea. Tamworth and Blossom turned to one another and smiled.

The Welsh Rabbit emerged cautiously with Mr. Rab and Hedgecock.

"A narrow squeak, indeed to goodness," he sighed.

"And Mr. Rab's a narrow pipsqueak," Hedgecock snorted, laughing at his own joke.

Chapter Twelve

*

Tamworth sat outside the "Duck and Drake", talking to certain officials and reporters about the proposed new route that the motorway should take. The bull-dozers and earth-movers had been halted while various important and high-up personages decided what to do.

Several of Tamworth's friends were there, and refreshment was laid on, beer and cheese and pickled onions from the inn, or coffee and biscuits from the Vicar's wife.

"Yes, I'm expecting a telegram from the Minister at any time now," Tamworth said. "He promised to send one as soon as a decision was reached."

Tamworth looked very pale and his eyes were dull. His ears hung heavily. He nibbled at an apple without enthusiasm.

"Where's Blossom? She's not here. In fact, I haven't seen her all week."

"Oh, she's up to something. She's got that I-know-something-you-don't look on her face. I kicked her yesterday because of it, the silly, fat thing," Thomas said.

"You're horribly mean to Blossom," Mr. Rab pro-tested. "I think she's the nicest girl in the world."

"And I think she's the stupidest," Thomas replied.

A telegraph boy came along the road on his red bicycle.

"Here comes the telegram," Tamworth said.

A Land-Rover was also coming from the other direction with Blossom waving from the front seat, but Tamworth's eyes were fixed on the telegraph boy, who seemed to have developed a puncture, for he had dismounted and was gazing solemnly at his front tyre. Some people ran forward to meet him, but Mr. Rab had been watching the Land-Rover.

He called out excitedly. "It's Blossom! And Farmer Baggs! They're getting out. And there's someone else with them. Oh! Oh! Oh! It's Melanie. It's Melanie. It's love."

Out of the Land-Rover, Blossom beaming at her side, came the pretty little black and pink pig, her plump form wobbling delightfully as she trotted straight towards Tamworth, who sat motionless as if he had been struck by lightning.

A reporter was rushing towards Tamworth, pulling the telegraph boy with him, but the pig had no eyes for them. His ears had pricked up, his eyes were shining and his bristles sparkled. Blossom ran to him and threw her arms round him.

"I had to fetch her. You were so thin and unhappy. I wrote to her farmer and he wrote to Farmer Baggs and then we went to fetch her. Oh, Tamworth, I'm so happy."

"Open the telegram. See what it says! Come on!"

Everyone was milling around Tamworth, who was
gazing into Melanie's eyes and gulping.

"I'm too old for you. You want a handsome, young
pig."

"You're the handsomest and cleverest pig in the
whole world. I want you, and I'm not going away
again. Never!"

She turned to Thomas.

"And I know you're Tamworth's friend and please, oh, please, Thomas, please like me."

She put out a black trotter on Thomas's arm and looked at him with her round, black snout and bright eyes. A grin spread slowly over his face.

"I love you," carolled Mr. Rab falling at her feet.

"It might work out," Hedgecock sniffed. "But for pity's sake READ THAT TELEGRAM!"

Tamworth's trotters were trembling wildly, so Blossom opened the envelope. He read it, shook his head in disbelief and then started to laugh, a great, huge, enormous, gigantic, tremendous, colossal, belly-shaking laugh that made him ripple from top to toe. Soon everyone else was laughing too.

"What are we laughing at?" Thomas said, still spluttering five minutes later.

"The wood is saved," Tamworth said.

The crowd cheered.

"But—but—the new route is to go right through the orchard and Pig House."

The crowd groaned.

"Why are you laughing then?" Thomas asked.

"I think it's funny that I did all that work to have it moved right through my house instead. I don't think I'll interfere next time."

"What are you going to do?"

"We shall do what we can to have it altered yet again, if only for the sake of Farmer Baggs's land. But, as for myself . . ."

He stretched his golden body till he seemed bigger than any pig that ever lived.

"Where Melanie is, where my friends are, that is my home, wherever it may be!"

Cheers rang out and he turned to go with his little pink and black pig and Blossom and Thomas.

"He doesn't half carry on," Hedgecock said to Mr. Rab. "All I can see is more work and trouble."

"And your trouble is that there's no poetry nor love in your soul. In fact, I doubt if you've got a soul. Don't hit me."

But Hedgecock hit Mr. Rab several times as they trotted along the way, following Tamworth Pig and the others.

Chapter Thirteen

———————————*———————————

"For goodness sake, Thomas, sit down."

"I can't."

"Well, stop wandering round the room. Read a book or play a game."

Daddy was being very patient for him, but Thomas continued to shuffle up and down, round and round.

"Look, boy, if you don't settle, you'll have to go to bed."

"I can't go to bed until I know."

"There's nothing to worry about. Piglets are being born all the time."

"But not Tamworth's piglets. They're special."

"Look at Blossom. She's just as excited as you are and she's sitting quietly reading."

Blossom stood up.

"I've read the same page twenty times and it still doesn't mean anything. Oh, Mummy, when shall we know?"

"It won't be long now. Come on, I'll make a drink and then you really will have to go to bed. It's almost midnight."

"I want to know how many," Thomas insisted.

"So do I," put in Hedgecock. "Fancy counting all those little trotters. Very interesting."

They all adjourned to the kitchen, including Daddy, and sat around the table.

"I can't wait," Thomas said.

"You say that every Christmas Eve. That's what tonight feels like, waiting for Christmas Day really to arrive. Or birthdays," Blossom replied.

Daddy stood up and yawned.

"Well, I'm off to bed and I think it would be a good idea if everyone else did, too."

He peered especially hard at Thomas.

"Please let us stay. Oh, Please. Please! PLEASE!"

"Farmer Baggs promised us he'd come," Thomas cried.

A loud knock rat-tatted at the door. The children rushed to open it and Farmer Baggs entered the kitchen, blinking in the bright light.

"I could see your lights were still on, so I thought I'd best let young Thomas and Blossom in on it."

"How many? How many? How many?" They danced round him.

Farmer Baggs's eyes were twinkling.

"Guess."

"Oh, no, don't tease us," Blossom cried.

"Eight," Thomas said.

Farmer Baggs shook his head.

"Ten," guessed Hedgecock.

"Fourteen," Thomas said, jumping up and down.

"No."

"Oh!" wailed Blossom. "There's only a few!"

"No, said Farmer Baggs.

"Eighteen," Thomas said, hopping on one leg.

"I give up. I can't bear it," Blossom whispered.

"I know! I know! I know!" Thomas shouted. "It's twenty, isn't it? Twenty piglets!"

Farmer Baggs nodded. "You're right, young Thomas."

"Twenty. Good heavens!" Mummy exclaimed.

Daddy went to a cupboard and brought out a bottle.

"Let's drink to the piglets, all twenty of them."

He filled up glasses for everyone. They raised them high.

"To Melanie, Tamworth and the twenty piglets," he toasted.

"To Melanie, Tamworth and the twenty piglets," they all replied.

Blossom's eyes shone like twin beacons.

"It's as good as Christmas."

"Better," Thomas shouted, turning a somersault on the floor.

"Mind now, I 'ope it stays at twenty."

Farmer Baggs's voice was serious.

"Why, what do you mean?" Mummy asked, full of quick concern.

"That last little un's very weak. It's the runt of the litter, all right, and it'll 'ave to be bottle-fed if it's to live. As a matter o' fact, we thought it was dead. Wasn't breathing at all. But Tamworth gave it the kiss o' life, and 'e kept on and on, 'e wouldn't give up 'ope, and in the end it gave a twitch and we wrapped un in a warm blanket and there it was, alive."

"Oh, poor little thing. Will it live?"

"I 'ope so, as otherwise, it's going to upset Tamworth summat terrible. 'E already thinks the world of that little black runt, he do."

"Black?" Daddy asked.

"Yes. As black as coal."

"What colour are the others?"

"We . . . ell, there's so many. But the first's a great, big, golden pig like Tamworth and there's lots more like 'im, and then there's some black and pink uns and some just pink uns, like all the colours o' the rainbow they are, but there's only one all black un, the runt."

"Oh, I want to see them, now," Blossom said.

"No, definitely not. Melanie and the piglets will need their sleep." Mummy's voice was firm.

"And so do Tamworth and I. Scoot, scatter, be off. You can see them in the morning."

Daddy's voice was even firmer so they went upstairs.

"I shall compose an extremely long poem about this," Mr. Rab decided.

"Ugh," Hedgecock growled.

"I shan't sleep," Thomas announced, settling Num around him in bed, and was thereupon struck by a terrible thought.

"You don't think I ought to give my Num to that little black piglet, do you? I don't really want to, but . . ."

"Shouldn't think it'd be much use to anyone but you really," Hedgecock, ever practical, said.

"Oh, good," yawned Thomas and fell asleep.

But Blossom lay awake thinking of the piglets and worrying about a small, black one who might not live till morning.

Despite their late night, the children arose early and without stopping for breakfast, though Blossom grabbed several chocolate biscuits as she went, they set out in the chilly Spring morning. Four months had passed since Melanie came, four months since they'd heard that the motorway was to cleave its way through Baggs's Farm and over Pig House, four months for Tamworth of unending speeches and meetings and delivering leaflets, but he was now a Pig filled with the strength of ten pigs because at the end of each day, Melanie was there to greet him with her gentle voice and loving ways. She did not come out and assist him, Thomas and Blossom did that as of old, but she was always ready at Pig House to greet the successful or comfort the downhearted.

But in the end it was all worthwhile. The Minister for the Environment visited Tamworth and it was decided that the motorway should take the original route after all, the one first chosen, through the slag heaps and the low-lying marshlands to the east. So at the end of March the digging, the clearing and the vast upheavals that accompany motorways began. The farm, Pig House and the damson tree and all the neighbourhood were safe.

By now, Melanie was enormous. She could hardly walk on her tiny trotters.

"It'll be funny if they're April Fool piglets," Thomas said.

"I don't fancy that," Tamworth sniffed, looking down his snout.

As a matter of fact they were born on 31st March,

but only just. The little black one arrived about an hour before midnight.

Tamworth was waiting for them, ears a-prick, bristles a-shine. He lifted his trotter to his mouth and shushed but it wasn't necessary. Blossom and Thomas were so much on tiptoe their feet hurt. They held two carrier bags, packed earlier, full of grapes and apples and cabbages. Nervous and excited, they entered the extra room built on to Pig House by Farmer Baggs for Melanie and the Piglets.

And there lay Melanie on her side, eyes closed, and curled against her was a warm, breathing, smooth sea of little bodies, almost too many to count. Thomas and Blossom and Hedgecock and Mr. Rab knelt down to touch the soft warmth. Melanie opened her eyes and looked proudly at her numerous offspring and smiled at them all.

"They're all real and complete. Look at their ears," Blossom breathed.

"It's their tails I like," Thomas said, touching a golden one.

The Welsh rabbit had crept in quietly beside them. "Primroses and celandines from the animals in the wood, brought you, I have," he murmured.

"Thank you," Melanie said.

"Shut up a minute," interrupted Hedgecock, that ungracious animal. "Flowers is no good to anyone. You've made me go wrong in my counting. I keep getting nineteen. Unless you've got one tucked under your tail, Melanie."

"Tamworth will show you the other one," she said.

The Pig of Pigs led them to the next room. There, on Tamworth's own bed, nestled in a soft blanket, surrounded by hot water bottles, lay the tiniest, funniest, ugliest, little pig ever.

"He's very small," Blossom said in surprise.

"Half the size of the others," Thomas added.

"A third I should say," Hedgecock surmised.

"Do you think he'll live?" squeaked Mr. Rab.

Hedgecock kicked him but Tamworth hadn't heard, for he was gazing with immense pride at his microscopic son.

"I saved him, you know. And he'll grow up to be a fine, big, noble pig, you'll see!"

There was a funny little noise rather like a snort of laughter from the sleeping animal, that made them all start in surprise.

"I wonder," thought Blossom. "I wonder."